Classics For Kids

Sherlock Holmes
The Red-Headed League

re-told for children by

Mark Williams

Odyssey

ISBN: 978-1541029866

How old were you

when you

discovered Sherlock?

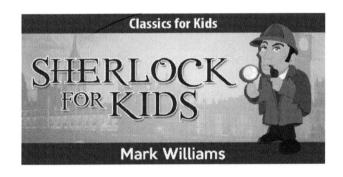

Sherlock For Kids on Facebook

Titles in this series include:

The Blue Carbuncle
Silver Blaze
The Red-Headed League
The Engineer's Thumb
The Speckled Band
The Six Napoleons
The Naval Treaty

Coming soon:

The Musgrave Ritual
The Beryl Coronet
The Gold Pince-Nez

The Red-Headed League 1

THERE IS NOTHING I like more than to take a stroll through London's parks when I have time to spare, and I especially love strolling through Regent's Park in the autumn.

And so it happened, one blustery October morning, that I was walking through Regent's Park on the way to Baker Street, the home of my dear friend Mr. Sherlock Holmes.

The trees were wearing their autumn colours – reds, browns, yellows and oranges, and all shades in between. Fallen leaves were being kicked about by happy ragamuffin children. The wind tugged playfully at my bowler hat, trying to blow it across the grass, but I kept one hand beside my head holding my bowler in place.

Unlike a gentleman about a hundred yards ahead of me, who I watched chasing his hat along the ground, blown along by gusts of wind every time he bent down to pick it up.

It reminded me of the case of the Blue Carbuncle the previous Christmas, when a lost bowler hat turned out to be the start of a bizarre mystery involving, of all things, a goose and a stolen jewel.

My dear friend Sherlock Holmes of course had soon got to the bottom of that little mystery, and as I meandered through Regent's Park that October morning I wondered when the next mystery might come along.

Little could I know the next mystery would be waiting for me the moment I arrived at 221b Baker Street.

The Red-Headed League 2.

I WAS REMINDED OF the colours of the falling leaves in Regent's Park when I opened the door and found Sherlock Holmes talking with a man who himself could best be described as autumnal.

The man had flaming red hair and a florid red face and crimson cheeks that, with his brown suit and shoes, made him look almost like the trees I had just left behind.

"I'm sorry, Holmes. I didn't realize you had visitors," I said. "I'll call back shortly."

"No, no," said Holmes. "Do come in, Watson. Do come in. I would like you to meet Mr. Jabez Wilson, who has just this evening come to me with a most bizarre mystery."

"Aha. This sounds interesting." I said. I put my hat and coat on the stand before stepping across to shake hands with Mr. Wilson.

Holmes turned to his guest. "Mr. Wilson, since you were only part way through your story, would you begin again and explain to my dear friend Dr. Watson the events that bring you here today. I will benefit from hearing the story again myself, it is so unusual."

At that moment Mrs. Hudson appeared in the doorway with a covered tray. She placed the tray on the table and removed the cloth to reveal a steaming pot of tea, milk and sugar, and three cups and saucers.

"I heard Doctor Watson arrive, Mr. Holmes," Mrs. Hudson said, "and I knew he would welcome a fresh pot of tea. Fortunately I already had the kettle on the stove, so the water was piping hot. And I knew your other guest had not yet left, so I took the liberty of adding a cup for him too."

"Splendid, Mrs. Hudson," Holmes declared. "You must be a mind-reader, for I was about to ring the bell and ask you to bring us some refreshments. Mr. Wilson, do help yourself to tea, and then take a seat and tell me again this quite remarkable story."

The Red-Headed League 3.

AFTER MRS. HUDSON had returned downstairs, I watched with interest as Mr. Jabez Wilson settled down in a chair and sipped his tea, gathering his thoughts before he began to tell his story.

I looked over the man, trying to apply the methods Sherlock Holmes had taught me, to deduce some facts about our guest. But other than that Mr. Wilson's clothes were old and shabby, and that his red face matched his red hair and that his short breaths and the fact that he was overweight suggested he was not in the best of health, I could tell nothing else.

Holmes had been watching me watching Mr. Wilson, and let out a sharp laugh. "Before you begin, Mr. Wilson, let us first hear what Dr. Watson has deduced about you."

Mr. Wilson looked at Holmes in surprise. "Deduced about *me*?"

Holmes smiled. "Watson has been learning some

of my methods. I find, Mr. Jabez Wilson, that one can tell a lot about a person by simply looking."

"Well, yes," agreed Mr. Wilson with a chuckle. "You can tell I am fat and have red hair, and my clothes are not new, so you might deduce I am not a rich man. But beyond that, I cannot imagine what anyone might conclude about me just by looking, good sir."

"I agree one cannot tell much in your case," Holmes said. He turned to me. "But I'm sure Watson noticed a few other trifling points. Isn't that so, Doctor Watson?"

"Well," I spluttered. "Obviously I saw that Mr. Wilson is, as he himself says, a little overweight and his clothes have seen better days. But apart from that, Holmes, I see nothing to remark upon."

Mr. Wilson splayed his hand in an *I told you so* fashion. "You see. Mr. Holmes, there is nothing whatsoever to deduce about me."

Holmes leaned back in his chair, stretched out his legs and crossed his arms."You are quite right, Mr. Jabez Wilson, of course," he said. "Other than that you were at one time a manual labourer – most likely a carpenter – and that you have been to China, oh and that you are right-handed and have done a lot of writing recently, I can deduce nothing about you whatsoever."

Mr. Wilson was opening and shutting his mouth like a goldfish. "Why, that is incredible," he said when he finally found his voice. "How on earth can you know all that? I have mentioned nothing of the kind in our conversation so far."

"It is simple enough," said Holmes. "Let's see. First there is the matter of your right hand."

"My right hand?" Mr. Wilson stared at his right hand as if he was seeing it for the first time. "What about my right hand?"

"One can tell a lot about a person by their hands, Mr. Wilson," Holmes said. "In your case your right hand is more muscular than the left, but the muscle is flabby, not firm. That told me several things about you."

"It did?" Mr. Wilson stared at Holmes, then at his own right hand again.

"It tells me both that you are right-handed and that you were once a manual labourer, probably a carpenter, but you no longer do woodwork," said Holmes.

Mr. Wilson's jaw dropped open. "That is correct in every detail," he said. "But how, Mr. Holmes? How?"

It was a question I was asking myself too. I should have spotted Mr. Wilson was right-handed , of course, as he held his cup with his right hand. With hindsight that was easy enough to deduce. But that Mr. Wilson was a manual labourer, and specifically a carpenter, but no longer did carpentry? That made no sense at all.

Or rather, it made no sense at all until Holmes explained it, at which point it was all embarrassingly obvious.

"That the right hand is more muscular than the left tells me you were a manual labourer," said Holmes. "Being right-handed you lift heavy objects with your right hand and that develops the muscles more than in the left hand."

"I see," said Mr. Wilson.

"But the fact that the muscle has become soft and flabby tells me you no longer do such work," Holmes continued.

"I see," said Mr. Wilson again.

"If you were a builder or a gardener your hands would be rough, but they are quite smooth, so I immediately thought of something like woodwork. A carpenter needs smooth hands to ensure the finished product is smooth and unblemished."

"Ah, but so does a potter," I said, seeing a flaw in Holmes's argument. "Someone working with clay would also need smooth hands, so could not Mr. Wilson have been a former potter or a former..." I tried to think of more examples of manual labour requiring smooth hands, but Holmes interrupted my thoughts.

"But what about his ears?" Holmes said.

The Red-Headed League 4.

MR. WILSON AND I BOTH stared at Holmes.

His ears? I thought.

"My ears?" Mr. Wilson said.

"I of course considered a number of possible trades that might explain the hands," said Holmes, "but it was Mr. Wilson's ears that clinched it for me that his former trade was that of a carpenter."

I looked at Mr. Jabez Wilson's ears. He had two of them, of course, one either side of his head, exactly where they ought to be, and both looked quite unremarkable. Neither big nor small. There was no sign saying these were carpenters' ears. What on earth was Holmes on about?

Mr. Wilson was obviously thinking the same thing. "What about my ears?" he asked.

"Your left ear is as nature intended, close to your head," explained Holmes, "but the top of the right ear sticks out a small way from the side of the head."

I looked again at Mr. Wilson's ears and saw this

was indeed the case.

"You are right, Holmes," I said, "but I am at a loss as to what this has to do with Mr. Wilson being a carpenter and not a potter."

"The carpenter's pencil," said Holmes matter-of-factly. "Carpenters use pencils to make marks on the wood they are working with, and they tend to slip the pencil behind their ear when not in use, to avoid it rolling away somewhere. Being right-handed Mr. Wilson of course slips his pencil behind his right ear, and after many years of doing just that we see the result – that the top of the right ear leans away from the side of the head."

Mr. Wilson had both hands to the sides of his head, his fingers testing how far each ear stuck out. He chuckled. "Right again, Mr. Holmes," he said. "But what about the writing? How on earth did you know I had done a lot of writing recently?"

"That was simple enough," said Holmes. "Your right sleeve between the cuff and the elbow is quite shiny, suggesting it has been rubbed against a table for long periods, as one does when writing a lot. Had it not been recently then the shine would have dulled with the passing of time. Also, you have slight ridge between your forefinger and middle finger from holding a pen for prolonged periods of time."

"It is all so obvious when you explain it, Mr. Holmes," said Mr. Jabez Wilson. "But China? How could you possibly know I have been to China?"

"Your tattoo, Mr. Wilson," said Holmes. "When

you leaned forward earlier to retrieve the newspaper from your pocket your sleeve rose a little and revealed a pink fish tattoo just above your wrist. It was quite fashionable a few years ago for visitors to China to get such a tattoo as a permanent souvenir of their visit."

Mr. Wilson chuckled again. "Let us hope you can use that fine mind of yours to make sense of the mystery I have brought you today then, Mr. Holmes," he said.

"I will try my best," said Holmes. "Mr. Wilson, will you show Dr. Watson the advertisement in that newspaper. Watson, will you read it out loud to me. I had already read it just before you arrived, but it will not hurt to hear it once more."

The Red-Headed League 5.

I TOOK THE NEWSPAPER from Mr. Wilson and read out loud the advertisement he had circled with a thick pencil. I wondered if it had been a carpenter's pencil.

"The Red-Headed League has a vacancy. Light work. Salary four pounds per week. Applicants must be over twenty-one and must have..."

I paused and read it to myself again first before repeating it out loud.

"And must have red hair."

I looked at Holmes. "Must have red hair? How extraordinary!"

"Indeed it is," agreed Holmes. "You will see the newspaper is dated two months ago. Mr. Wilson, will you explain to the doctor about your other business."

"Well, Dr. Watson," Mr. Jabez Wilson said to me, "it's like this. While I used to be a carpenter, as Mr. Holmes so correctly observed, I now run a small pawn-broker business here in London. It brings me in a little money each month, such as I can live comfortably, but of course a little extra cash is always welcome."

I nodded my agreement. I earned enough from my surgery to live more than comfortably, but my wife was always hinting how nice it would be if we had a little more coming in, so what Mr. Wilson said next came as no surprise to me.

"When I saw this advertisement for a job offering four whole pounds a week for a few hours light work, I naturally wanted to know more," he said. "As you see, I have a fine head of red hair, and I am obviously over twenty-one, so I thought to myself, why not?"

"Why not indeed," I said. "But how do you manage to run your own business if you are working a few hours each day at this job?"

"Well," said Mr. Wilson, "normally that would have been a problem, but quite by chance, about three months ago, a Mr. Vincent Spaulding came knocking on my door saying he was new to the area and that he wanted to learn a trade."

Holmes was leaning back in his chair, his eyes closed, listening carefully to Mr. Jabez Wilson's story. Without opening his eyes, he said, "Three months ago, Watson. That may be significant."

I shrugged my shoulders. I could see no significance whatsoever. I said to Mr. Wilson. "Let me get this quite straight, sir. This man Spaulding came to your door wanting you to train him as a carpenter?"

"No, no," laughed Mr. Wilson. "As a pawnbroker. Spaulding said he was very keen to learn about the business. So much so he offered to work for me for nothing if I would train him in how a pawnbroker business is run. All he wanted in return was that I let him stay in my spare room as he had nowhere to live, and that I provide meals for him."

"So of course you took him up on the offer," I said. "I think I would do the same if someone came knocking on my door offering to work for nothing. What about you, Holmes?"

Holmes smiled, his eyes still shut. "But I already have an assistant who works for me for free," he said. "And a very fine assistant you are too, Watson. But Mr. Wilson, pray continue your story."

"Well," said Mr. Wilson, "Spaulding started work for me the very next day, and I have to say I have no complaints whatsoever. He works hard during the day and keeps to his own room when the shop was shut, so I see very little of him. He has a hobby too. He is a photographer, and so I allow him the use of my empty cellar to use as a dark room to develop his film."

"What sort of photographs does he take?" Holmes asked.

Mr. Wilson thought for a few seconds, then said, "To be honest, Mr. Holmes, I have no idea. Photography is not a subject that at all interests me in any way, so I had no reason to ask. I myself am an avid philatelist. I collect stamps. But I would not expect anyone else to ask to see my collection. Each to his own. Mr. Holmes. Each to his own."

"So you never had occasion to go down to the cellar where Spaulding's films were being developed?" Holmes asked.

"Never," said Mr. Wilson. "In all the years I have lived in that house I have only been down to the cellar once, when I first moved in. There is plenty of space above ground, so I have no need of a cellar at all, and so I was quite happy to let Spaulding use it for his hobby."

"I quite understand," said Holmes. "Now, let us return to the matter of the strange advertisement in the newspaper. Tell Watson how you came to know about it."

"Ah yes," said Mr. Wilson. "Now this was a happy coincidence on two counts. First, had Spaulding not started to work for me the month before, I would not have been able to apply for this job that paid four pounds a week for a few hours work."

"That was indeed a happy coincidence," said Holmes. "But tell Dr. Watson here about the second happy coincidence."

The Red-Headed League 6.

MR. JABEZ WILSON TURNED to me again. "Well it was quite lucky for me that my employee reads the newspaper ads," he said. "One day we were enjoying a cup of tea together and Spaulding suddenly told me how he wished he had flaming red hair like I have."

"So he had seen the advertisement too," I said.

"In fact it was Spaulding who told me about it," explained Mr. Wilson. "Were it not for Spaulding I would never have seen the advertisement, never have heard of the Red-Headed League, I would not have been earning four extra pounds a week for almost two months, and I would not be here now seeking the advice of Mr. Holmes."

"As you say, two happy coincidences," I said. "Or perhaps I should say unhappy coincidences, for I gather something bad must have happened for you to be here this morning."

"Well actually, no, Dr. Watson," said Mr. Wilson. "Only in so far as I no longer have the job and therefore am no longer earning my extra four pounds a week. That's the strange thing. Nothing bad has happened. I applied for the job, got the job and was paid very well for my work."

"Then why are you here?" I wanted to know.

Holmes briefly opened one eye. "Perhaps, Watson, if you were to allow Mr. Wilson to continue his story, we will find out."

"Yes, sorry, Holmes," I said. "Do continue, Mr. Wilson."

Mr. Wilson finished his cup of tea, and settled back in his chair to tell me the next part of his story.

"No, the reason that I am here is that this matter is so bizarre I can make no sense of it whatsoever. Of course everyone knows of the reputation of Mr. Sherlock Holmes for solving mysteries, and while I this case there has been no crime committed, so far as I can tell, it is such a bizarre story I hoped Mr. Holmes might be able to shed some light on the matter for me."

"And very pleased I am that you came, Mr. Wilson, for this is indeed a most bizarre affair," said Holmes. "Now please, continue your story, and omit nothing, for I fear there is much more to this story than at first meets the eye. You were saying about how Spaulding drew your attention to the advertisement."

"Indeed," said Mr. Wilson. "Spaulding seemed to

know a little about this Red-Headed League. He told me this was not the first time the Red-Headed League had advertised. He explained to me that an eccentric American millionaire, himself red-haired, had left a vast sum of money in trust, and that it would be used solely to provide employment for men in London with flaming red hair."

"Extraordinary!" I exclaimed, leaning forward. "Quite extraordinary! And obviously you applied for and got the job."

"Much to my surprise," said Mr. Wilson. "When I arrived at the address given there was a long, long queue of red-headed men, many of whom had hair just as fiery as mine. To be honest I thought I had no chance, and almost walked away, but Spaulding had accompanied me, to where the interviews were taking place, and he encouraged me to stand in line until I had been interviewed."

"So Spaulding was doing his best to help you, Mr. Wilson, to pay you back for your helping him," I suggested.

"That was how I saw it," said Mr. Wilson.

"It is certainly one way of looking at things," said Holmes. "However there are other possibilities. But pray continue your story, Mr. Wilson."

"As I was saying," said Mr. Wilson, "Spaulding seemed quite confident I would get the job, and of course he was proved right. Luck was with me, and when I finally got to the office and was interviewed they offered me the post straight away."

"How many people interviewed you?" Holmes asked. "What kind of office was it?"

"Just the one," said Mr. Wilson. "A man in late thirties, I would guess, well-dressed, and balding a little. The office was not what I expected. Very sparsely furnished, with just one table and two chairs. Not even a wastepaper bin."

"Did you not think that a bit strange?" asked Holmes.

"I did," said Mr. Wilson, "but I remembered Spaulding had explained the Red-Headed League was the legacy of an eccentric American millionaire, and an office with just one table and two chairs seemed no more or less eccentric than offering a job paying four pounds a week to a person with red hair."

"What work did they want you to do?" I asked.

Holmes sat up, eyes open. "This," he said, "is what I am keen to learn too, for this was as far as Mr. Wilson had got explaining the matter to me you arrived, Watson. Pray, do go on, Mr. Wilson. What was it, exactly, that the Red Headed-League wanted you to do for four pounds a week?"

The Red-Headed League 7.

"THIS IS WHERE IT GETS very strange," said Mr. Wilson. "They said the hours would be ten in the morning until two in the afternoon. Just four hours a day. For four pounds a week! For that much money I would happily have undertaken work much more challenging than what they had in mind for me."

"Which was what?" Holmes asked impatiently.

"Bizarre, Mr. Holmes. Quite bizarre," Mr. Wilson said. "They wanted me to copy out, word for word, the *Encyclopaedia Britannica*!"

"Just that?" I asked.

"Just that," said Mr. Jabez Wilson.

We all fell silent for a moment, letting this news sink in.

Then Holmes asked, "Did they by any chance insist you remained at the office for the full four hours while you did this work?"

"Why, yes they did," said Mr. Wilson. "You have heard of the Red-Headed League before, then?"

"Never," said Holmes quietly, "but a certain picture is emerging."

"Well, you are quite right, Mr. Holmes," Mr. Jabez Wilson said. "I was told that if I left the office at any time during my work hours then I would lose the job and the pay. But this was not a problem for me. I worked each day for the full four hours, and received my four pounds every week."

"Let me get this straight," I said. "They actually paid you for copying out the Encylopaedia Britannica?" I asked. "Four pounds a week?"

"Exactly so," said Mr. Wilson. "I started at A and copied out each entry onto a sheet of paper. Sometimes it was very boring, but other times quite interesting. I learned new things I had never known before, about aardvarks, and Amsterdam, and Argentina..."

"Very educational for you," said Holmes.

"But what possible benefit did this Red-Headed League get from your doing this?" I asked. "Why would anyone pay you anything, let alone four whole pounds a week, for copying out a book?"

Mr. Jabez Wilson shrugged. "That is quite beyond me, Dr. Watson. But whatever reason, it seems no longer to be important, for today it all stopped."

The Red-Headed League 8.

"STOPPED?" HOLMES SAT forward in his chair, rubbing his hands gleefully. "Now this is most interesting. Do go on."

"Well, that's why I'm here, Mr. Holmes," said Mr. Jabez Wilson. "I arrived at the office this morning only to find the place locked, and a notice pinned to the door saying the Red Headed-League was closed."

"How strange," I said.

"I enquired among the other offices in the building but no-one seemed to know anything about the Red-Headed League," said Mr. Wilson. "It seems someone had rented the office for just two months, paid cash in advance. They did mention a name but I quite forget now what it was."

"No matter," said Holmes. "The name would have been a false one anyway."

"A false name?" Mr. Wilson stared at Holmes. "Why would they have given a false name?"

"My dear fellow," said Holmes. "Of course it

would be a false name. This is a serious matter," Holmes said solemnly.

"It most certainly is," agreed Mr. Wilson. "Why, I have lost four pounds a week!"

Sherlock Holmes laughed out loud at this. "Better to look on it that you gained four pounds a week for two months, Mr. Wilson."

Mr. Jabez Wilson did not look too happy with this point of view.

"No, what bothers me now," said Holmes, "is what these people were really up to."

Mr. Wilson stared at Holmes. "What they were really up to?"

"Well it must be obvious to us all that this Red-Headed League was some deliberate invention," said Holmes, "and there never was any red-headed American millionaire, eccentric or otherwise, leaving money to fellow red-headed men."

"That much I have worked out for myself, Mr. Holmes," said Jabez Wilson. "But why? Why on earth would anyone play such a bizarre joke on me? And to pay me four pounds a week for almost eight weeks to do so… It makes no sense. No sense whatsoever."

Holmes was deep in thought. Suddenly he got up and went to his bookshelf. He took down a map of London and spread it on the table.

"Show me exactly where your pawnbroker's shop is," he said.

Mr. Wilson got up and pointed out the road to Holmes.

"Excellent," said Holmes. "Very close to Aldersgate tube station. That will save us some time, Watson." To Mr. Jabez Wilson he said, "Describe Mr. Vincent Spaulding to me. No, even better. I will describe Spaulding to you and you will tell me if I am right or wrong. I am guessing Spaulding is about thirty years old, clean-shaven, with a white acid mark on his forehead, and pierced ears."

Mr. Wilson was doing his impression of a goldfish again, opening and shutting his mouth but unable to find the words.

Eventually he said, "That is him, Mr. Holmes. So you know Spaulding then?"

"I had never heard of Vincent Spaulding until you arrived here," said Holmes.

"Then how?" Mr. Wilson wanted to know.

"Later," said Holmes. For now, just to be clear, while you were busy at this office copying out the *Encyclopaedia Britannica,* your employee, the man you know as Vincent Spaulding was looking after your own business unsupervised," said Holmes.

"Well, yes," said Mr. Wilson, "but I have no concerns there. I know my stock well, and it is all intact. There is no money on the premises other than the daily takings. So far as I can tell, Vincent Spaulding did his work each day in my absence, just as he did when I was there in person. I have no reason to think Spaulding was stealing from me."

"I am quite certain Vincent Spaulding stole nothing from *you*," said Holmes. "Now, today is Friday. Is Vincent Spaulding working at the shop this morning?"

"He is," said Mr. Wilson.

"Might I ask, Mr. Wilson," said Holmes, "that you do not return to your shop for the next few hours."

"If you think it will help you, Mr. Holmes, certainly," said Mr. Wilson. "I have some other business in the city to attend that will take me through until late afternoon, by which time Spaulding will have shut the shop for the weekend and be up in his room reading, or down in the cellar developing his photographs."

"Splendid," said Holmes. "On Monday I fear you will have to look after your shop on your own again, for one way or another Spaulding will no longer be working for you."

"Really?" said Mr. Wilson. "I shall be sorry to see him go."

"Perhaps you will see things differently on Monday morning, when everything is explained to you," said Holmes. "But for now, Mr. Wilson, I suggest you get along and do whatever business you have to do. Watson and I are going to take a little stroll ourselves, and we both have a busy evening ahead."

The Red-Headed League 9.

"WELL, WATSON, WHAT do you make of it all?" Holmes asked me after Mr. Jabez Wilson had left.

"I confess I can make nothing of it whatsoever, Holmes," I said. "It is all quite bizarre. Why would anyone pay a man four pounds a week to copy out a book? And what did you mean, we have a busy evening ahead?"

"Let us go out a while," said Holmes. "I could do with some fresh air."

We put our hats and coats on, but only for a brief few minutes did we enjoy the fresh air, for no sooner had Holmes led me out of 221b Baker Street than we went straight to Baker Street tube station and down onto the London Underground, where we took a train to Aldersgate.

As is his way. Holmes explained nothing to me on the journey. He preferred to keep his ideas to himself until he was quite certain about something, and I knew there was no point in me asking him questions.

I would find out soon enough why we were going to Aldersgate Station.

We reached street level again at Aldersgate, and after a short walk Holmes stopped outside a particular shop.

"Here we are," Holmes said.

I looked up and was surprised to find we were outside a pawnbroker's shop, and the painted sign above the window declared *Mr. Jabez Wilson, Esq. Pawnbroker*. I thought we were perhaps heading for the office where Mr. Wilson has been copying out the Encyclopaedia Britannica, but instead we had come to Mr. Wilson's home.

I was even more surprised when Holmes suddenly began thumping his walking stick on the pavement. Not once, not twice, but three times. Then he walked down the road and up again, looking at the shops and buildings either side. I watched with interest, but could not imagine what Holmes might be thinking.

Then Holmes came back to Jabez Wilson's pawnbroker's shop and rapped loudly on the door. After a few moments a man appeared who could only be Vincent Spaulding, for he exactly matched the description Holmes had given earlier, right down to the pierced ears.

Then came the third surprise.

"I am looking for the butcher's shop, my man," said Holmes.

I stared at Holmes.

Vincent Spaulding stared at Holmes.

"Does this look like a butcher's shop?" Spaulding jerked his thumb down the road. "It's down that way." He slammed the door shut before Holmes even had a chance to say thank you.

"A-hah," I said to Holmes. "I am with you this time. You aren't looking for a butcher's shop at all. You did that just to see Spaulding's face and confirm it was the man you described earlier."

"Actually," said Holmes, "I was already quite certain who it was."

"Then why?" I wanted to know.

"It was not his face I wanted to see," said Holmes. "It was his knees."

The Red-Headed League 10.

HIS KNEES? I STARED AT Holmes, but I knew there was no point in asking. Holmes would explain when he was good and ready. Not before.

Holmes waltzed off down the road and I scurried after him. I realised Holmes was deliberately taking long strides and counting them as he went, so I said nothing for fear of breaking his concentration.

We walked around the corner and up the next road that ran parallel behind the road where the Jabez Wilson pawnbroker's shop had been. Again Holmes started taking long strides and counting as he went along. Then he suddenly stopped and, with scant regard for horses and carriages hurrying back and forth with their passengers, Holmes crossed the road and stood on the pavement on the other side.

"I commend the view from here, Watson," Holmes shouted across at me.

I dodged a Hackney carriage and rushed across to where Holmes stood. I turned to see what was so interesting, but was disappointed to find there was nothing but the usual row of shops one might expect.

"Um, Holmes," I said, "what exactly am I supposed to be looking at?"

"This street runs parallel to the street where Jabez Wilson has his pawnbroker's shop," said Holmes, as if this explained everything.

"What of it?" I asked.

"If my pacing is correct, then as the crow flies we are almost exactly in line with where Mr. Jabez Wilson's shop is on the parallel road," said Holmes.

I looked around for a crow, but all I could see were London pigeons. "I saw a raven in Regent's Park this morning," I said helpfully. "And of course the black swans on the Serpentine."

Holmes laughed. "My dear fellow, what I mean is, were a crow to fly straight from here and across the buildings opposite us and then continue flying, the next street it would cross would be Mr. Wilson's street, and very likely it would exactly fly over Mr. Wilson's shop."

I stared at Holmes. In all my years as a friend of Sherlock Holmes I had never know him take the remotest interest in where birds flew. Least of all crows when there were no crows to be seen.

Holmes saw my look of bewilderment and said, "Tell me what you see."

"Horses and carriages on the road," I said. "Shoppers walking on the pavement. That sort of thing. Nothing at all unusual for a late Friday morning."

"What about the buildings opposite," said Holmes.

I studied the buildings carefully, as obviously this was something Holmes regarded as important, but I could not see why.

"There is a tobacconist, a newsagent, a bank, a carriage-repair shop and a vegetarian restaurant," I said. "No butcher's shop, though."

"No, no," Holmes chuckled. "My interest in the butcher's shop was just a ploy to see Spaulding's knees, remember? No, it is this line of shops that is of particular interest to us."

I looked again at the shops, one by one. Why on earth would these be of particular interest?

A tobacconist? Holmes smoked a pipe, much to my disgust, but he always bought his tobacco from the local tobacconist in Baker Street.

A newsagent? Holmes had the newspapers delivered daily to his door so he could read them over breakfast while still wearing his favourite purple dressing gown.

A bank? Why would this particular bank interest Holmes? His own bank was on Baker Street, just a few minutes walk from his rooms.

A carriage-repair shop? Holmes didn't own a carriage, let alone one in need of repair.

As for a vegetarian restaurant... Holmes was far too fond of goose and pheasant, venison and pork, to ever go to a vegetarian restaurant.

Holmes looked back at me. "It will all make sense

very early tomorrow morning," he said. "But right now, Watson, I suggest you go home and get some rest. I would like you to meet me at 221b Baker Street at ten o'clock tonight for a little adventure."

"Adventure?" I said.

"Oh," Holmes added. "And bring your pistol with you, Watson. We will be dealing with dangerous men."

The Red-Headed League 11.

OF COURSE I DID NOT get much rest, for I spent the remainder of the day trying to make sense of it all.

I knew that everything Holmes had seen and heard, I had seen and heard.

I had been there when Mr. Wilson Jabez explained the bizarre Red-Headed League affair, and I was there when Holmes went to Aldersgate Station afterwards.

I was there when Vincent Spaulding answered the door, and I was there when Holmes thumped his stick on the pavement.

I was there when Holmes paced the street and then did the same in the parallel road.

I had seen the same row of shops that Holmes had seen.

The difference between us being, that I had seen nothing out of the ordinary that entire morning other than the strange advert in the newspaper from two months ago, and the fact that Mr. Jabez Wilson had been paid four pounds a week to copy out the *Encyclopaedia Britannica.*

But I could not for the life of me see what that had to do with Spaulding's knees, thumping pavements with a walking stick, and a row of shops consisting of a tobacconist, a newsagent, a bank, a carriage-repair shop and a vegetarian restaurant.

As for being told to return to Baker Street at ten o-clock and to bring my gun because we would be dealing with dangerous men...

Well, if anyone else but Sherlock Holmes had said that I would have thought them utterly crazed and I would have stayed at home with my dear wife.

But I knew Holmes well enough to understand that if Holmes said I should bring my pistol because we would be dealing with dangerous men then, in all likelihood, we would be dealing with dangerous men and I would need my pistol.

The Red-Headed League 12.

I ARRIVED AT 221B BAKER Street just before ten o'clock, and saw two Hansom cabs outside. Holmes was in the hall way waiting for me, accompanied by a police detective I knew, Mr. Peter Jones, and a well-dressed gentleman in a top hat who I had never seen before.

Holmes introduced the stranger as Mr. Merryweather and said that he was banker, but I was still none the wiser as to why he was there with us, or what Holmes had planned for us.

And I got the impression neither the police detective, Mr. Peter Jones, nor the banker, Mr. Merryweather, were sure either.

We took the two Hansom cabs and crossed the gas-lit streets of London. When we stopped I was most surprised to find we were in Aldersgate again, in the same road Holmes had led us to earlier in the day. The road that ran parallel behind the street where

Mr. Jabez Wilson had his pawn-broker's shop.

I was even more surprised when Mr. Merryweather produced some keys from his pocket and let us into a side-door of the bank. The same bank that was in the middle of the row of shops we had been looking at earlier.

Well, that at least told me that the tobacconist, the newsagent, the carriage-repair shop and the vegetarian restaurant were not what Holmes had been interested in.

But why would Holmes want to visit a bank so late at night? Why was the bank's owner there? And why was Mr. Jones, the police detective there?

Mr. Merryweather led us down into the secure vault below the bank, where there were a number of empty wooden crates piled up but otherwise nothing to be seen.

"I have done as you asked, Mr. Holmes," said Mr. Merryweather, "and removed all the valuables to another place. Although I am still mystified as to why you wanted this done."

"All in good time, Mr. Merryweather," said Holmes. "If you will be patient a short while you will soon see why it was necessary, and why I have asked Detective Jones to join us." He turned to the detective. "Are your men all in position, Jones?" he asked.

"Everything has been arranged according to your instructions," said Mr. Jones "although I am quite as confused as Mr. Merryweather here as to what you expect to happen."

"Not long to wait now," said Holmes. He dropped to the ground with his lamp and began examining the cracks between the flagstones with his magnifying glass. We all looked on in astonishment as Holmes crept around the floor on his hands and knees.

"All is well," he said when he finally stood up. "Now, we must sit quietly for an hour or two." He extinguished his lamp. "Total silence, please, and total darkness. No lamps or matches. Oh, and Jones, have your cuffs to hand, and Watson, have your pistol ready. We will need them."

The Red-Headed League 13.

WE SAT FOR AN HOUR OR two in the dark and silence. It was cold in the bank vault, but even so I found myself almost drifting off to sleep. But I stayed awake somehow, trying to work out what on earth Holmes expected to happen.

Then, at about two o'clock the next morning, it all began to make sense, for suddenly a chink of light appeared in the darkness. And quite unexpectedly the light appeared in the ground, between the flagstones!

As we watched, fascinated, the chink of light became a strip of light the length of the crack and then, to my astonishment, the crack of light became a rectangle of light as the flagstone was pushed up and moved across, grating noisily.

Then a hand appeared. I gripped my pistol firmly. I knew my companions were sitting quietly nearby, hidden by the darkness, and they would be ready to take whatever action was necessary, but I was the only one with a pistol.

A second hand appeared on the edge of the hole left by the moved flagstone and I watched, pistol ready, as a head appeared in the rectangle of light shining up from below. The head became a body as a man hauled himself out onto the floor of the bank vault. Behind him the hand of a second man appeared, ready to climb out.

The first man, by now almost all the way out of the hole, was holding a gun. Holmes shot forward from the darkness and struck the man's hand with his walking stick, knocking the weapon to the ground. I ran across, pointing my pistol at the man.

"Stay where you are or I will fire!" I shouted.

"It's a trap! Run for it!" the man screamed to his partner.

The police detective Peter Jones sprang forward to grab the second man, but all he got hold of was the man's coat, as the villain dropped back down into the tunnel and disappeared.

"The games over, John Clay," said Holmes to the first man. He held the villain firmly by the shoulders while Detective Peter Jones brought out handcuffs and cuffed the intruder called John Clay.

Mr. Merryweather struck a match and lit his lamp, and by the lamp's light I saw that the intruder John Clay had a distinctive white acid mark on his forehead, and pierced ears. It was the same Vincent Spaulding I had seen at Mr. Jabez Wilson's pawnbroker's shop when Holmes had rapped on the door and asked about the butcher's shop.

Spaulding, or Clay as I should now call him, recognized Holmes in the same instant.

"You," he sneered. "The one that asked about the butcher's shop."

Holmes smiled back. "Sherlock Holmes at your service," said Holmes.

Detective Jones stared at Holmes. "Butcher's shop?" he said.

"It's a long story," said Holmes.

"Your friend won't get far, John Clay," said Detective Jones. "I have officers at the other end waiting for him as he tries to leave."

Mr. Merryweather looked on in amazement. "Mr. Holmes, how can I ever thank you? Were it not for you, the bank would have lost the entire French gold bullion we had stored here."

The Red-Headed League 14.

WE HELPED DETECTIVE Jones escort John Clay up to the street, where uniformed officers were waiting to take the villain away to the police station for further questioning. I guessed he would be spending along time in prison.

"Did you get the other man?" Detective Jones asked them.

"Yes, guv," said one of the officers. "He's already on his way to the station. He ran straight into our arms at the other end of tunnel, in the cellar of the pawnbroker's shop, just as Mr. Holmes said would happen"

"Mr. Jabez Wilson's pawnbroker's shop?" I asked. "So they tunneled from Wilson's cellar to here. Then this is all connected with the Red-Headed League somehow." Detective Jones, Mr. Merryweather and the other police officers all stared at me.

"The what-headed league?" they said in unison.

"The other man must be the person who

interviewed Mr. Jabez Wilson and gave him the job," I said.

John Clay glared at Holmes. "It looks like you've got everything worked out."

Holmes chuckled. "It was a cunning plan, Clay, I give you that," said Holmes. "But you were greedy. Four pounds too greedy."

"What do you mean?" growled John Clay.

"Simply this," said Holmes. "Had you paid Mr. Jabez Wilson for one more day's work, instead of shutting down the Red-Headed League on the Friday morning as soon as the tunnel was finished, then Mr. Wilson would not have come to me with his bizarre story until Monday at the earliest, and by then you would have made your getaway with the French gold bullion and very likely be on the continent and never have been caught."

Detective Jones stepped forward. "Men, take John Clay away, and I'll meet you at the station later."

We watched the officers cart John Clay away.

"Mr. Merryweather," continued the detective, "I'll have two men standing guard either end of the tunnel until you can make arrangements later today to have it filled in and have your vault restored to its normal condition. I will come and see you Monday morning and explain exactly what happened, once I know myself."

Detective Jones turned to Holmes. "Mr. Holmes and Dr. Watson, if you are heading back to Baker Street now I will join you and you can explain to me how on earth you could possibly have known about this bank robbery in advance. Oh, and you can also explain to me what on earth the Red-Headed League is."

The Red-Headed League 15.

AT THAT TIME OF morning there were only a few two-passenger cabs available so we had to get two separate cabs, and the explanations had to wait until we were all safely back at 221b Baker Street.

Once there I explained to Mr. Jones the part of the story I knew, telling the detective about Mr. Jabez Wilson's visit, about the newspaper advertisement and the Red-Headed League and the job paying four pounds a week to copy out the Encyclopaedia Britannica, and how everything had suddenly stopped that Friday morning. By the time I had finished I was growing tired and I fear my story was becoming a little garbled.

"Then Mr. Jabez Wilson left us and we took the tube to Aldersgate," I concluded. "Holmes thumped his walking stick on the pavement, asked Spaulding where the butcher's shop was so he could see Spaulding's knees, and then we looked at the tobacconist and the vegetarian restaurant and

Holmes told me to bring my pistol at ten o'clock."

Holmes chuckled. "The one thing that was obvious from the start was that this Red-Headed League had only one purpose," Holmes said. "To get Mr. Jabez Wilson out of his own shop so these villains could do their dirty work."

"I see that now," I said. "And obviously the photography hobby of Vincent Spaulding, alias John Clay, was in fact nothing more than an excuse for him to be down in the cellar all the time."

"That's right," said Holmes. "From that information I suspected a tunnel was being dug, and when I knocked on the door of the shop and Spaulding answered, I checked his knees and shoes for tell-tale signs of digging, which confirmed my theory. But it didn't tell me where the tunnel was going."

"That's why you thumped your stick on the pavement outside," I said. "By doing that you deduced that the tunnel was not at the front of the building, but at the back."

"Which was why we then walked around to the next street parallel," said Holmes, "and I commented on the variety of shops there."

"Including the bank," I said. "That's why counted your paces along the street, so you could see where the tunnel would lead from the rear of the Jabez Wilson shop."

"As the crow flies," said Holmes. "It was obvious it could only be to one of those five shops I drew your attention to, and of course no-one would ever want to tunnel into a newsagent's or a tobacconist's."

"Or a carriage repair shop or a vegetarian restaurant," I laughed. "So it had to be the bank."

"I had read in the papers that that particular bank had just taken storage of some precious gold bullion," said Holmes, "so after you left for home, Watson, I contacted the bank's directors, and of course Detective Jones here, and made the necessary arrangements to move the gold to safety and have us waiting for the villains."

"But how did you know that it would be tonight?" I asked.

"Well, the fact that the Red-Headed League had been shut down told me that the men had finished the tunnel," said Holmes. "There was no point in paying Jabez Wilson another four pounds a week to keep him away once that tunnel was dug."

"Of course," said I. "That's what you meant when you told Clay he had been four pounds too greedy. But why tonight? How did you know it would be tonight and not another night? Tomorrow, for example?"

"I think I can guess one reason," said Detective Jones, not wanting to be left out. "Obviously Clay and his partner knew that the longer the tunnel was there the more chance someone might accidentally find it. Supposing Mr. Jabez Wilson, for example, had decided for some reason to go down to his cellar over the weekend."

"That makes sense," I said. "Anything else, Holmes?"

"That's simple enough," said Holmes. "By attempting the robbery on the Friday night, once the bank had closed for the weekend, Clay knew that he would have two clear days to get the gold bullion safely stashed away before the bank opened the vault on the Monday morning and discovered the theft."

"And were it not for you, Mr. Sherlock Holmes, that's exactly what would have happened," said Detective Jones, shaking Holmes by the hand.

I reached out and shook my friend by the hand too.

"Sherlock Holmes," I said, "you make it all sound so simple. I congratulate you on another mystery solved."

The End.

Thank you for reading.

Thank you for reading *Sherlock Holmes re-told for children : The Red-Headed League,* one of the *Classics For Kids : Sherlock Holmes* short story adaptations of the Sir Arthur Conan Doyle classics.

If you enjoyed it, please leave a review and tell your friends

There is a list at the end of this book of all titles currently available in *Classics For Kids : Sherlock Holmes* series. Plenty more to come!

Classics For Kids : Sherlock Holmes ebooks are available from all good ebook retailers worldwide and can be read on smartphones, tablets and e-readers.

Paperback and audio-book versions are also available.

There are lots more *Sherlock For Kids* titles on the way. To get updates on when new titles in this series are released, and for other new releases by this author, just email to

markwilliamsauthor@gmail.com

and ask to be put on the mailing list for *Classics For Kids : Sherlock Holmes* updates.

All author proceeds from the *Sherlock For Kids* series go towards supporting babies, children, families and schools in The Gambia, West Africa.

The
Classics For Kids : Sherlock Holmes
Series

The following titles are now available as ebooks from all good ebook retailers worldwide and may also be available as paperbacks and audio-books.

The Blue Carbuncle
Silver Blaze
The Red-Headed League
The Engineer's Thumb
The Speckled Band
The Six Napoleons
The Naval Treaty

**Sherlock Holmes Re-told for Children
3-in-1**
The Blue Carbuncle
Silver Blaze
The Red-Headed League

**Sherlock Holmes Re-told for Children
3-in-1**
The Engineer's Thumb
The Speckled Band
The Six Napoleons

**Sherlock Holmes Re-told for Children
6-in-1**
The Blue Carbuncle
Silver Blaze
The Red-Headed League
The Engineer's Thumb
The Speckled Band
The Six Napoleons

Coming next:

The Musgrave Ritual
The Beryl Coronet
The Gold Pince-Nez

Made in the USA
Columbia, SC
14 September 2020